THE PENGUIN POETS

THE RETRIEVAL SYSTEM

Born in Philadelphia in 1925, Maxine Kumin earned her B.A. and M.A. degrees from Radcliffe College. She has lectured in English at Princeton, Brandeis, Columbia, and other universities. In addition to the present volume, she is the author of five collections of poetry, four novels, and a number of children's books, some of these last written with her friend Anne Sexton. In 1972 she received *Poetry* magazine's Eunice Tietjens Memorial Prize, and in 1973 her *Up Country: Poems of New England* was awarded the Pulitzer Prize. Having lived for many years in Newton Highlands, Massachusetts, a suburb of Boston, she and her husband now reside year-round on their farm in New Hampshire.

ALSO BY MAXINE KUMIN

THE RETRIEVAL SYSTEM

POEMS BY

MAXINE KUMIN

PENGUIN BOOKS

Penguin Books Ltd, Harmondsworth,
Middlesex, England
Penguin Books, 40 West 23rd Street,
New York, New York 10010, U.S.A.
Penguin Books Australia Ltd, Ringwood,
Victoria, Australia
Penguin Books Canada Limited, 2801 John Street,
Markham, Ontario, Canada L3R 1B4
Penguin Books (N.Z.) Ltd, 182–190 Wairau Road,
Auckland 10, New Zealand

First published in the United States of America
in simultaneous hardcover and paperback editions by
The Viking Press and Penguin Books 1978
Paperback edition reprinted 1979, 1984

LIBRARY OF CONGRESS CATALOGING IN PUBLICATION DATA
Kumin, Maxine W.
   The retrieval system.
   I. Title.
PS3521.U638R4   1978b   811'.5'4   78–2465
ISBN 0 14 042.258 7

Printed in the United States of America by
The Book Press, Brattleboro, Vermont
Set in Linotype Caledonia

ACKNOWLEDGMENTS

Harper & Row, Publishers, Inc.: "Hello, Hello Henry" from *Up Country*
by Maxine Kumin. Copyright © Maxine Kumin, 1970.
Reprinted by permission of Harper & Row, Publishers, Inc.

Grateful acknowledgment is made to the following publications,
in which these poems first appeared:

The American Poetry Review: "Making the Connection," "Changing the Children,"
"Body and Soul: A Meditation," and "The Grace of Geldings in Ripe Pastures";
The American Review: "Seeing the Bones"; *Atlantic Monthly:* "The Retrieval Sys-
tem" and "The Food Chain"; *Chicago Review:* "Waiting Inland"; *Folger Shake-
speare Library:* "Tonight"; *Harvard Magazine:* "Caught"; *Inscape:* "A Mortal
Day of No Surprises"; *A Local Muse:* "Territory"; *Mademoiselle:* "Progress Re-
port"; *Mother Jones:* "My Father's Neckties"; *The New Republic:* "Remember-
ing Pearl Harbor at the Tutankhamen Exhibit"; *The New Yorker:* "How It Is,"
"Splitting Wood at Six Above," "Henry Manley, Living Alone, Keeps Time," "July,
Against Hunger," and "The Longing to Be Saved"; *Poetry:* "The Excrement
Poem," "In April, in Princeton," and "The Archaeology of a Marriage"; *Poetry
Now:* "Address to the Angels"; *Quest/77:* "Sunbathing on a Rooftop in Berkeley"
and "The Survival Poem"; *The Real Paper:* "The Henry Manley Blues."

For my daughters

Contents

The Retrieval System

It begins with my dog, now dead, who all his long life
carried about in his head the brown eyes of my father,
keen, loving, accepting, sorrowful, whatever;
they were Daddy's all right, handed on, except
for their phosphorescent gleam tunneling the night
which I have to concede was a separate gift.

Uncannily when I'm alone these features
come up to link my lost people
with the patient domestic beasts of my life. For example,
the wethered goat who runs free in pasture and stable
with his flecked, agate eyes and his minus-sign pupils
blats in the tiny voice of my former piano teacher

whose bones beat time in my dreams and whose terrible breath
soured *Country Gardens, Humoresque,* and unplayable Bach.
My elderly aunts, wearing the heads of willful
intelligent ponies, stand at the fence begging apples.
The sister who died at three has my cat's faint chin,
my cat's inscrutable squint, and cried catlike in pain.

I remember the funeral. *The Lord is my shepherd,*
we said. I don't want to brood. Fact: it is people who fade,
it is animals that retrieve them. A boy
I loved once keeps coming back as my yearling colt,
cocksure at the gallop, racing his shadow
for the hell of it. He runs merely to be.
A boy who was lost in the war thirty years ago
and buried at sea.

Here, it's forty degrees and raining. The weatherman
who looks like my resident owl, the one who goes out and in
by the open haymow, appears on the TV screen.
With his heart-shaped face, he is also my late dentist's double,
donnish, bifocaled, kind. Going a little gray,
advising this wisdom tooth will have to come out someday,
meanwhile filling it as a favor. Another save.
It outlasted him. The forecast is nothing but trouble.
It will snow fiercely enough to fill all these open graves.

1 MAKING THE CONNECTION

The Longing to Be Saved

When the barn catches fire
I am wearing the wrong negligee.
It hangs on me like a gunny sack.
I get the horses out, but they
wrench free, wheel, dash back
and three or four trips are required.
Much whinnying and rearing as well.
This happens whenever I travel.

At the next stopover, the children take off
their doctor and lawyer disguises
and turn back into little lambs.
They cower at windows from which flames
shoot like the tattered red cloth
of dimestore devil suits. They refuse
to jump into my waiting arms, although
I drilled them in this technique, years ago.

Finally they come to their senses and leap
but each time, the hoop holds my mother.
Her skin is as dry and papery
as a late onion. I take her
into my bed, an enormous baby
I do not especially want to keep.
Three nights of such disquiet
in and out of dreams as thin as acetate

until, last of all, it's you
trapped in the blazing fortress.
I hold the rope as you slide from danger.
It's tricky in high winds and drifting snow.

Your body swaying in space
grows heavier, older, stranger

and me in the same gunny sack
and the slamming sounds as the gutted building burns.
Now the family's out, there's no holding back.
I go in to get my turn.

Address to the Angels

Taking off at sunset over the city
it seems we pull the sun up
and pin it over the rim
or is it the other way round,
is it the horizon we push down
like a loose cuticle?
I am up here grieving, tallying
my losses, and I think how once
the world was flat and rested on
the back of a giant fish whose tail
was in his mouth and on the Day
of Judgment all the sinners fell
overboard into the black gulf.
Once, we walked distances
or went by horse and knew our places
on the planet, gravity-wise.

Now angels, God's secret agents,
I am assured by Billy Graham,
circulate among us to tell
the living they are not alone.
On twenty-four-hour duty, angels
flutter around my house and barn
blundering into the cobwebs,
letting pots boil over
or watching the cat torture
a chipmunk. When my pony
filching apples, rears and catches
his halter on a branch and hangs
himself all afternoon, I like
to think six equine angels fan

the strangling beast
until his agony is past.

Who knows how much or little
anyone suffers? Animals
are honest through their inability
to lie. Man, in his last hour,
has a compulsion to come clean.
Death is the sacred criterion.
Always it is passion that
confuses the issue. Always
I think that no one
can be sadder than I am.
For example, now, watching
this after after-sunset
in the sky on top of Boston
I am wanting part of my life back
so I can do it over.
So I can do it better.

Angels, where were you when
my best friend did herself in?
Were you lunching beside us
that final noon, did you catch
some nuance that went past my ear?
Did you ease my father out
of his cardiac arrest that wet
fall day I sat at the high crib bed
holding his hand? And when
my black-eyed susan-child ran
off with her European lover

and has been ever since an unbelonger,
were you whirligiging over
the suitcases? Did you put
your imprimatur on
that death-by-separation?

It's no consolation, angels,
knowing you're around
helplessly observing like
some sacred CIA. Even
if you're up here, flattened
against the Fasten Your Seatbelt sign
or hugging the bowl in the lavatory,
we are, each one of us, our own
prisoner. We are
locked up in our own story.

My Father's Neckties

Last night my color-blind chainsmoking father
who has been dead for fourteen years
stepped up out of a basement tie shop
downtown and did not recognize me.

The number he was wearing was as terrible
as any from my girlhood, a time of
ugly ties and acrimony: six or seven
blue lightning bolts outlined in yellow.

Although this was my home town it was tacky
and unfamiliar, it was Tehran or Gibraltar
Daddy smoking his habitual
square-in-the-mouth cigarette and coughing
ashes down the lightning jags. He was
my age exactly, it was wordless, a window
opening on an interior we both knew
where we had loved each other, keeping it quiet.

Why do I wait years and years to dream this outcome?
My brothers, in whose dreams he must as surely
turn up wearing rep ties or polka dots clumsily
knotted, do not speak of their encounters.

When we die, all four of us, in
whatever sequence, the designs
will fall off like face masks
and the rayon ravel from this hazy version
of a man who wore hard colors recklessly
and hid out in the foreign
bargain basements of his feelings.

Waiting Inland

Here, there is no escaping
the telephone poles that pin
the grass to the sky until
on the horizon's seam, ten
tumbleweeds, faceless porcupines,
come humming toward me

but when my grandfather lived
I rode to the end of the line
in Ocean City, where the motormen's
black lunchboxes hung open
in the roundhouse like old
galoshes and I stuffed thumbs
in my ears as metal bit metal
on the turntable.

Consider a hundred motel rooms
with the grit of distant sidewalks
ground into the carpet. Flinch from
the rattle of useless drawers
holding in their Gideon Bibles.
Hear the wet flint of ice cubes
and the cacophony of toilets
that suck back like the Atlantic tides.

I wait in such a place remembering
what it is to be young and hungry.
What it is to skulk under the boardwalk
or sprawl on the beach out of season.
I remember how in my French book
everyone was exhorted, *à Paris, à Paris!*

Once, I picked my mosquito bites
and ate the scabs like sea salt
and was unreasonably happy
on the porch of my grandfather's house
where all night outside the ribcage
of my bed a ghost hand stage-managed
the green wicker rockers, and time
lay down to sleep like an exhausted puppy.

Making the Connection

Looking for good news to skate out with
over the ice pond of sleep, I'm tricked instead
to think I hear him whimpering in the kitchen.
His ghost comes on metal toenails,
scratches himself, the thump of thighbone
on linoleum. Ghost laps water. Whines. Soon
he will howl in the prison of his deafness,
that paranoid, strangled sound
waking the grown children who all live elsewhere.

I sit up, breaking the connection
like hanging up on my brother.

I am ten. I go down terrified
past a houseful of bubbling breathers,
unlatch the cellar door, go further
down in darkness to lie on old carpet
next to the incontinent puppy.
His heartbeat, my heartbeat comfort us
and the fluttering pulse of the furnace
starting up, stopping, and the vague
percussion of pipes that buzz
in the far corner.

Brother,
Brother Dog, is that who you were?
Is that who I was?

The Eight-Hour Dance

The night the shift key locked
on my typewriter
and I was at the mercy
of capital letters
a heron marched off the platen
on his unwieldy gear.
The paper birches undressed.
My mare came into the kitchen
and took off her sharp shoes
one by one
and with my index fingernail
I etched I LOVE YOU
on the foolscap of your back.

In the morning
waking to the mortal scratch
I saw bats rise
out of your mustache.
A clutch of snails
humped from your ears.
The good fairy had put
a parachute under your pillow
and thus you flew off.

I was content
to read such omens
like the twelve years
of Chinese Chance
until this moment. Now
I need to know who you are,
lover, and what dance
we danced.

Progress Report

The middle age you wouldn't wait
for now falls on me, white
as a caterpillar tent, white
as the sleetfall from apple trees
gone wild, petals that stick
in my hair like confetti
as I cut my way through clouds
of gnats and blackflies in the woods.

The same scarlet tanager
as last year goes up, a red
rag flagging from tree to tree,
lending a rakish permanence to
the idea of going on without you

even though my empty times
still rust like unwashed dogfood cans
and my nights fill up with porcupine
dung he drops on purpose at
the gangway to the aluminum-
flashed willow, saying that
he's been here, saying he'll come
back with his tough waddle, his pig eyes,
saying he'll get me yet. He is
the stand-in killer I use
to notarize your suicide
two years after, in deep spring.

Thomas Mann's permit to take
refuge in Switzerland said:

"for literary activities and
the passage of life's evening."
I wonder if all those he loved
and outlived showed up nights
for chips of reconstructed
dialogue under the calm Alps,
he taking both parts, working it out.
Me taking both parts in what
I suppose is my life's afternoon.

Dear friend, last night I dreamed
you held a sensitive position,
you were Life's Counselor
coming to the phone in Vaud or Bern,
some terse one-syllable place,
to tell me how to carry on

and I woke into the summer solstice
swearing I will break
your absence into crumbs
like the stump of a punky tree
working its way down
in the world's evening
down to the forest floor.

2 HENRY MANLEY

Hello, Hello Henry

My neighbor in the country, Henry Manley,
with a washpot warming on his woodstove,
with a heifer and two goats and yearly chickens,
has outlasted Stalin, Roosevelt and Churchill
but something's stirring in him in his dotage.

Last fall he dug a hole and moved his privy
and a year ago in April reamed his well out.
When the county sent a truck and poles and cable,
his Daddy ran the linemen off with birdshot
and swore he'd die by oil lamp, and did.

Now you tell me that all yesterday in Boston
you set your city phone at mine, and had it ringing
inside a dead apartment for three hours
room after empty room, to keep yours busy.
I hear it in my head, that ranting summons.

That must have been about the time that Henry
walked up two miles, shy as a girl come calling
to tell me he has a phone now, 264, ring two.
It rang one time last week—wrong number.
He'd be pleased if one day I would think to call him.

Hello, hello Henry? Is that you?

The Food Chain

The Hatchery's old bachelor, Henry Manley
backs his pickup axle-deep into my pond
opens the double tub of brookies
and begins dipping out his fingerlings.
Going in, they glint like chips of mica.

Henry waits a while to see them school up.
They flutter into clumps like living rice grains.
He leaves me some foul-smelling pellets
with instructions how to sow them on the water
a few days until they smarten and spread out.

What *he* does is shoot kingfishers with his air rifle.
They ate two thousand fry on him last weekend.
Herons? They hunt frogs, but watch for martens.
They can clean a pond out overnight.
He stands there, busy with his wrists, and looking savage.

Knowing he knows we'll hook his brookies
once they're a sporting size, I try for something
but all the words stay netted in my mouth.
Henry waves, guns the engine. His wheels spin
then catch.

Extrapolations from Henry Manley's Pie Plant

The stalks are thick as cudgels, red
as valentines, a quarter-acre bed

planted thirty years before
Henry even toddled out of doors.

It's June. *A man of eighty-two's
too old to mow a lawn this size,* he says

meanwhile mowing. I agree, and pick.
We both know Henry's seventy-six

but people tend to brag agewise
bending the facts whichever way they choose

and the braggers-up, it seems to me,
can be forgiven the more easily.

I look at my middling self and recognize
this life is but one of a number of possible lives.

I could have studied law or medicine,
elected art history, gambled, won

or lost. I could have opened out each evening
in a downtown bar, all mirrors and singing.

Instead, mornings I commence with the sun,
tend my animals, root in the garden

and pass time with Henry. Goldfinches explode
from the meadow where thistle's the mother lode

as I follow a map no wider in landscape
than the path the wild sorrel takes.

Bearing armloads of Henry's rhubarb away,
humbly I will return him a pie or two

and when the chipmunks litter their October
feed lots with hickory husks, a home-cured

pickup full of horse manure, to let
its goodness leach out slowly in that bed

meanwhile thanking whatever's thankable
that acting on Henry's rich example

I'm to boast a hundred or so Junes
of pie plant and yellow bird and the mare's bloodlines.

The Henry Manley Blues

Henry Manley's house, unpainted for
eighty years, shrinks as attached sheds crease
and fold like paper wings. An elm tree sheers
the sitting porch off in a winter storm.
And Henry's fields are going under, where
the beavers have shut down a local stream
flooding his one cash crop, neat rows of pines
he'd planned to harvest for Christmases to come.
Their tips are beanpoles now, sticking up through ice.
We skate on the newborn pond, we thump on the roof
of the lodge and squat there, listening for life.

*Trouble with this country is, there's more
beavers than people in it.* Henry gums
milk toast experimentally, still sore
from the painless dentist who emptied out his mouth.
*Trouble is, these Conservation bums
—they're only kids, y'know, with blasting caps—
they'd rather blow the dam up than set traps,
traps is* work. *By damn! They'll drive me out.*

Measurers live here, rat-shaped and tough,
with cutting tools for teeth and tails that serve
as plasterers' trowels. Where aspen's not enough
they go to birch and apple rather than starve.
Whatever tree they fell they cut the wood
in thirty-six-inch lengths. They're rarely off
that mark more than an inch or two. And what
they don't build with they store for winter food.

Henry hears their nightwork from his bed.
His phantom teeth are killing him again.
Traps! You got to trap the kit inside!
Layer by layer the lodge is packed with mud
and board by batten his view of things falls in.

Henry Manley, Living Alone, Keeps Time

Sundowning,
the doctor calls it, the way
he loses words when the light fades.
The way the names of his dear ones
fall out of his eyeglass case.
Even under the face of his father
in an oval on the wall
he cannot say *Catherine, Vera, Paul*
but goes on loving them out of place.
Window, wristwatch, cup, knife
are small prunes that drop from his pockets.
Terror sweeps him from room to room.
Knowing how much he weighed once
he knows how much he has departed his life.
Especially he knows how the soul
can slip out of the body unannounced
like that helium-filled balloon
he opened his fingers on, years back.

Now it is dark. He undresses
and takes himself off to bed
as loose in his skin as a puppy,
afraid the blankets will untuck,
afraid he will flap up, unblessed.
Instead, proper nouns return to his keeping.
The names of faces are put back
in his sleeping mouth. At first light
he gets up, grateful once more

for how coffee smells. Sits stiff
at the bruised porcelain table
saying them over, able
to with only the slightest catch.
Coffee. Coffee cup. Watch.

3 THE ENVELOPE

Birthday Poem

I am born at home
the last of four children.
The doctor brings me as promised
in his snap-jawed black leather satchel.

He takes me out in sections
fastens limbs to torso
torso to neck stem
pries Mama's navel open
and inserts me, head first.

Chin back, I swim upward
up the alimentary canal
bypassing mouth and nose holes
and knock at the top
of her head to be let out
wherefore her little bald spot.

Today my mother is eighty-two
splendidly braceleted and wigged.
She had to go four times to the well
to get me.

Changing the Children

Anger does this.
Wishing the furious wish
turns the son into a crow
the daughter, a porcupine.

Soon enough, no matter how
we want them to be happy
our little loved ones, no
matter how we prod them
into our sun that it may
shine on them, they whine
to stand in the dry-goods store.
Fury slams in.
The willful fury befalls.

Now the varnish-black son in a tree
crow the berater, denounces the race
of fathers, and the golden daughter
all arched bristle and quill
leaves scribbles on the tree bark
writing how The Nameless One
accosted her in the dark.

How put an end to this cruel spell?
Drop the son from the tree with a rifle.
Introduce maggots under his feathers
to eat down to the pure bone of boy.

In spring when the porcupine comes
all stealth and waddle to feed on the willows
stun her with one blow of the sledge
and the entrapped girl will fly out

crying Daddy! or Danny!
or is it Darling?
and we will live all in bliss
for a year and a day until
the legitimate rage of parents
speeds the lad off this time
in the uniform of a toad
who spews a contagion of warts
while the girl contracts to a spider
forced to spin from her midseam
the saliva of false repentance.

Eventually we get them back.
Now they are grown up.
They are much like ourselves.
They wake mornings beyond cure,
not a virgin among them.
We are civil to one another.
We stand in the kitchen
slicing bread, drying spoons,
and tuning in to the weather.

Parting

Each year in the after-Christmas tinsel
of the airport lounge you see them
standing like toys that have been
wound up once or twice and then
shunted aside. Mother, father,
whose bodies time has thickened
to pudding, resolute daughter,
stylish and frightened.
That small a constellation,
that commonplace a grouping.

They are done with speaking.
They do not weep.
They do not touch one another except
after the final boarding call
when they are fastened all
three as in a dangerous struggle
exploding only as she
is drawn into the silver belly of the jet
and shot from the parents
and this is the celestial arrangement.

Seeing the Bones

This year again the bruise-colored oak
hangs on eating my heart out
with its slow change, the leaves at last
spiraling end over end like your
letters home that fall Fridays
in the box at the foot of the hill
saying the old news, keeping it neutral.
You ask about the dog, fourteen years
your hero, deaf now as a turnip,
thin as kindling.

In junior high your biology class
boiled a chicken down into its bones
four days at a simmer in my pot,
then wired joint by joint
the re-created hen
in an anatomy project
you stayed home from, sick.

Thus am I afflicted, seeing the bones.
How many seasons walking
on fallen apples like pebbles in
the shoes of the Canterbury faithful
have I kept the garden up
with leaven of wood ash, kitchen leavings
and the sure reciprocation of horse dung?

How many seasons have the foals
come right or breeched or in good time
turned yearlings, two-year-olds, and at three
clattered off in a ferment to the sales?

Your ponies, those dapple-gray kings
of the orchard, long gone to skeleton,
gallop across the landscape of my dreams.
I meet my father there, dead years before
you left us for a European career.
He is looping the loop on a roller coaster
called Mercy, he is calling his children in.

I do the same things day by day.
They steady me against the wrong turn,
the closed-ward babel of anomie.
This Friday your letter in thinnest blue
script alarms me. Weekly you grow
more British with your *I shalls*
and now you're off to Africa
or Everest, daughter of the file drawer,
citizen of no return. I give
your britches, long outgrown, to the crows,
your boots with a summer visit's worth
of mud caked on them to the shrews
for nests if they will have them.

Working backward I reconstruct
you. Send me your baby teeth, some new
nail parings and a hank of hair
and let me do the rest. I'll
set the pot to boil.

The Archaeology of a Marriage

When Sleeping Beauty wakes up
she is almost fifty years old.
Time to start planning her retirement cottage.
The Prince in sneakers stands thwacking
his squash racquet. He plays
three nights a week at his club
it gets the heart action up.
What *he* wants in the cottage
is a sauna and an extra-firm Beauty-
rest mattress, which *she* sees as an exquisite
sarcasm directed against her long slumber.
Was it *her* fault he took so long
to hack his way through the brambles?
Why didn't he carry a chainsaw
like any sensible woodsman?
Why, for that matter, should any
twentieth-century woman
have to lie down at the prick of
a spindle etcetera etcetera
and he is stung to reply
in kind and soon they are at it.

If only they could go back to
the simplest beginnings. She
remembers especially a snapshot
of herself in a checked gingham outfit.
He is wearing his Navy dress whites.
She remembers the illicit weekend
in El Paso, twenty years before
illicit weekends came out of the closet.
Just before Hiroshima

just before Nagasaki
they nervously straddled the border
he an ensign on a forged three-day pass
she a technical virgin from Boston.
What he remembers is vaster:
something about his whole future
compressed to a stolen weekend.
He was to be shipped out tomorrow
for the massive land intervention.
He was to have stormed Japan.
Then, merely thinking of dying
gave him a noble erection.

Now, thanatopsis is calmer
the first ripe berry on the stem
a loss leader luring his greedy
hands deeper into the thicket
than he has ever been.
Deeper than he cares to be.
At the sight of the castle, however
he recovers his wits and backtracks
meanwhile picking. Soon his bucket
is heavier etcetera than ever
and he is older etcetera
and still no spell has been recast
back at Planned Acres Cottage.
Each day he goes forth to gather
small fruits. Each evening she stands
over the stewpot skimming
the acid foam from the jam

expecting to work things out
awaiting, you might say, a unicorn
her head stuffed full of old notions
and the slotted spoon in her hand.

Sunbathing on a Rooftop in Berkeley

Eleven palm trees stand up between me
and the Bay. A quarter turn and I'm
in line with Campanile Tower.
The hippies are sunbathing too.
They spread themselves out on the sidewalks
with their ingenious crafts for sale
and their humble puppies. We are
all pretending summer is eternal.
Mount Tamalpais hovers in the distance.

I pinch myself: that this is California!
But behind my lightstruck eyelids I am also
a child again in an amusement park
in Pennsylvania, and forty years blow
in and out adapting, as the fog does,
to conditions in the Bay.

My daughter has gone to her class in Criminal
Procedure. She pulls her hair back in a twist.
Maybe she will marry the young man she lives with?
I take note how severely
she regards the laws of search and seizure.
She moves with the assurance of a cheetah.
Still, marriage may be the sort of entrapment
she wishes to avoid? She is all uncertainties,
as I am in this mothering business.

O summers without end, the exact truth is
we are expanding sideways as haplessly
as in the mirrors of the Fun House.
We bulge toward the separate fates that await us

sometimes touching, as sleeves will, whether
or not a hug was intended.

O summers without end, the truth is
no matter how I love her, Death
blew up my dress that day
while she was in the egg unconsidered.

The Envelope

It is true, Martin Heidegger, as you have written,
I fear to cease, even knowing that at the hour
of my death my daughters will absorb me, even
knowing they will carry me about forever
inside them, an arrested fetus, even as I carry
the ghost of my mother under my navel, a nervy
little androgynous person, a miracle
folded in lotus position.

Like those old pear-shaped Russian dolls that open
at the middle to reveal another and another, down
to the pea-sized, irreducible minim,
may we carry our mothers forth in our bellies.
May we, borne onward by our daughters, ride
in the Envelope of Almost-Infinity,
that chain letter good for the next twenty-five
thousand days of their lives.

4 BODY AND SOUL

Body and Soul: A Meditation

Mornings, after leg lifts and knee bends,
I go up in a shoulder stand.
It's a form of redress. My
winter melancholy hangs
upside down. All my organs
reverse their magnetic fields:
ovaries bob on their eyestalks,
liver, kidneys, spleen, whatever
is in there functioning unseen,
free-float like parachutes,
or so it seems from plough position,
legs behind my head, two
big toenails grazing the floor.

Body, Old Paint, Old Partner,
I ought to have paid closer
attention when Miss Bloomberg
shepherded the entire fifth grade
into the Walk-Through Woman.
I remember going
up three steps, all right,
to enter the left auricle.
I remember the violet light
which made it churchly
and the heartbeat amplified
to echo from chamber to chamber
like God speaking unto Moses.

But there was nothing about the soul,
that miners' canary flitting
around the open spaces;

no diagram in which
the little ball-bearing soul
bumbled her way downhill
in the pinball machine
of the interior, clicking
against the sternum,
the rib cage, the pelvis.
The Walk-Through Woman ceased
shortly below the waist.
Her genitals were off limits.

Perhaps there the soul
had set up housekeeping?
Perhaps a Pullman kitchen,
a one-room studio
in an erogenous zone?
O easy erogenous zones!
Flashing lights, detour
and danger signs in
the sprouting pubic hair.
Alas, I emerged from
the right ventricle
little the wiser.

Still unlocated, drifting,
my airmail half-ounce soul
shows up from time to time
like those old-fashioned
doctors who used to cheer
their patients in girls' boarding schools
with midnight bedside visits.

Body, Old Paint, Old Partner
in this sedate roundup we ride,
going up the Mountain in
the meander of our middle age
after the same old cracked tablets,
though soul and we touch tongue,

somehow it seems less sure;
somehow it seems we've come
too far to get us there.

How It Is

Shall I say how it is in your clothes?
A month after your death I wear your blue jacket.
The dog at the center of my life recognizes
you've come to visit, he's ecstatic.
In the left pocket, a hole.
In the right, a parking ticket
delivered up last August on Bay State Road.
In my heart, a scatter like milkweed,
a flinging from the pods of the soul.
My skin presses your old outline.
It is hot and dry inside.

I think of the last day of your life,
old friend, how I would unwind it, paste
it together in a different collage,
back from the death car idling in the garage,
back up the stairs, your praying hands unlaced,
reassembling the bites of bread and tuna fish
into a ceremony of sandwich,
running the home movie backward to a space
we could be easy in, a kitchen place
with vodka and ice, our words like living meat.

Dear friend, you have excited crowds
with your example. They swell
like wine bags, straining at your seams.
I will be years gathering up our words,
fishing out letters, snapshots, stains,
leaning my ribs against this durable cloth
to put on the dumb blue blazer of your death.

Splitting Wood at Six Above

I open a tree.
In the stupefying cold
—ice on bare flesh a scald—
I seat the metal wedge
with a few left-handed swipes,
then with a change of grips
lean into the eight-pound sledge.

It's muslin overhead.
Snow falls as heavy as salt.
You are four months dead.
The beech log comes apart
like a chocolate nougat.
The wood speaks
first in the tiny voice
of a bird cry, a puppet-squeak,
and then all in a rush,
all in a passionate stammer.
The papery soul of the beech
released by wedge and hammer
flies back into air.

Time will do this as fair
to hickory, birch, black oak,
easing the insects in
till rot and freeze combine
to raise out of wormwood cracks,
blue and dainty, the souls.
They are thin as an eyelash.
They flap once, going up.

The air rings like a bell.
I breathe out drops—
cold morning ghost-puffs
like your old cigarette cough.
See you tomorrow, you said.
You lied.
We're far from finished! I'm still
talking to you (last night's dream);
we'll split the phone bill.
It's expensive calling
from the other side.

Even waking it seems
logical—
your small round
stubbornly airborne soul,
that sun-yellow daisy heart
slipping the noose of its pod,
scooting over the tightrope,
none the worse for its trip,
to arrive at the other side.

It is the sound
of your going I drive
into heartwood. I stack
my quartered cuts bark down,
open yellow-face up.

Late Snow

It's frail, this spring snow, it's pot cheese
packing down underfoot. It flies out of the trees
at sunrise like a flock of migrant birds.
It slips in clumps off the barn roof,
wingless angels dropped by parachute.
Inside, I hear the horses knocking
aimlessly in their warm brown lockup,
testing the four known sides of the box
as the soul must, confined under the breastbone.
Horses blowing their noses, coming awake,
shaking the sawdust bedding out of their coats.
They do not know what has fallen
out of the sky, colder than apple bloom,
since last night's hay and oats.
They do not know how satisfactory
they look, set loose in the April sun,
nor what handsprings are turned under
my ribs with winter gone.

The Excrement Poem

It is done by us all, as God disposes, from
the least cast of worm to what must have been
in the case of the brontosaur, say, spoor
of considerable heft, something awesome.

We eat, we evacuate, survivors that we are.
I think these things each morning with shovel
and rake, drawing the risen brown buns
toward me, fresh from the horse oven, as it were,

or culling the alfalfa-green ones, expelled
in a state of ooze, through the sawdust bed
to take a serviceable form, as putty does,
so as to lift out entire from the stall.

And wheeling to it, storming up the slope,
I think of the angle of repose the manure
pile assumes, how sparrows come to pick
the redelivered grain, how inky-cap

coprinus mushrooms spring up in a downpour.
I think of what drops from us and must then
be moved to make way for the next and next.
However much we stain the world, spatter

it with our leavings, make stenches, defile
the great formal oceans with what leaks down,
trundling off today's last barrowful,
I honor shit for saying: We go on.

Remembering Pearl Harbor at the
Tutankhamen Exhibit

Wearing the beard of divinity, King Tut
hunts the hippopotamus of evil.
He cruises the nether world on the back
of a black leopard. And here he has put
on his special pectoral, the one
painted with granulated gold. This will
adorn him as he crosses over.
                          I shuffle
in line on December seventh to see
how that royal departure took place.
A cast of thousands is passing this way.
No one looks up from the alabaster
as jets crisscross overhead. Our breaths
cloud the cases that lock in the gold
and lapis lazuli.
                    The Day
of Infamy, Roosevelt called it. I was
a young girl listening to the radio
on a Sunday of hard weather. Probably
not one in seven packed in these rooms
goes back there with me.
                          Implicit
throughout this exhibit arranged
by Nixon and Sadat as heads of state
is an adamantine faith
in total resurrection.
Therefore the king is conveyed
with a case for his heart
and another magnificent

hinged apparatus, far too small,
for his intestines, all in place,
all considered retrievable

whereas if one is to be blown
apart over land or water
back into the Nothingness
that precedes light, it is better
to go with the simplest detail:
a cross, a dogtag,
a clamshell.

In April, in Princeton

They are moving the trees in Princeton.
Full-grown and burlapped, aboard two-ton
trucks, great larches go up the main artery
—once the retreat route of Washington's army—
to holes in the ground I know nothing of.
They are moving the trees for money and love.

They are changing the grass in Princeton
as well. They are bringing it in from sod farms
rolled tight as a church-wedding carpet, unrolled
on the lawn's raw skin in place of the old
onion grass, acid moss, dandelions.
The eye rests, approving. Order obtains.

There is no cure for beauty so replete
it hurts in Princeton. In April, here's such light
and such benevolence that winter
is overlooked, like bad table manners.
Peach, pear, and cherry bloom. The mockingbirds
seize the day, a bunch of happy drunkards

and mindful it will pass, I hurry each noon
to yoga in the Hillel Reading Room
where Yahweh and Krishna intersect in Princeton;
where, under my navel in lotus position
by sending fresh *prana* to the center
albeit lunchless, the soul may enter.

Here, let me not forget Antonin Artaud
who feared to squat, lest his immortal soul
fly out of his anus and disappear

from the madhouse in thin air.
Let me remember how I read these words
in my square white office, its windows barred

by sunlight through dust motes, my own asylum
for thoughts unsorted as to phylum.
Cerulean-blue rug softening the floor,
desk, chair, books, nothing more
except for souls aloft—Artaud's, perhaps,
and mine—drifting like the waxy cups

of white magnolias that drop their porcelain
but do not shatter, in April, in Princeton.

5 THE TIME ON EITHER SIDE OF NOW

Caught

Late August. The goats keep leaving Eden.
Identical twin Toggenburgs, they swim
to freedom, climb tree stumps; maybe they fly?
While I boil my hands red skinning beets
their collar bells sound, distant telephones.
Intercepting the call, I go with grain
to rattle in a coffee can. One
has got an ancient pea vine in her mouth.
The other trails a plate-size bloom of squash.
When they circle me, wary but gluttonous,
I pounce, snaring one, which flops like a great warm fish
against my breasts, then stiffens, then goes limp.
I carry her off to her fenced half-acre. Meanwhile
the other, perfectly cloned, trots at my side
and interjects staccato sounds of displeasure
—at not being carried? At the genetic misfortune
of having to duplicate her sister's act?
They give me a Bronx cheer send-off, scoot
to the top of the boulder ridge, long hidden
in raspberry cane, now eaten clean, and forget
for a day or two how they came out in the world.

Late August. Truce, this instant, with what's to come.
Everything caught. This moment caught. My horse
at the paddock fence making that soft
ingratiating nicker that asks for supper.
No older and no riper than was planned
the sun staining the west. My matching hands.

57

Tonight

Tonight the peepers are as loud as all
the grandmothers of the world's canaries, those
Petey- and Dicky-birds trilling vibratos
from their baggage-handle perches, perpetual
singing machines stoned on seeds of finches' hemp.

Tonight the peepers are a summer camp-
ful of ten-year-olds still shrilling after taps.
Winter will have us back with cold so harsh
the nose hairs freeze. Weasels will spring the traps.
But tonight—tonight the peepers raise the marsh.

July, Against Hunger

All week the rain holds off. We sweat
stuffing the barn full, like a pillow,
as much as it will hold of these
strangely dead, yellow cubes we set
in unchinked rows, so air can move between.
The smell collects, elusive, sweet,
of gray nights flicked with the snake tongue
of heat lightning, when the grownups sat
late on the side porch talking politics,
foreclosures, war, and Roosevelt.

Loneliness fills me like a pitcher.
The old deaths dribble out. My father clucks
his tongue, disapproving of manual labor.
I swivel to catch his eye, he ducks
behind the tractor, his gray fedora
melts into this year's colt munching grain.
Meanwhile, a new life kicks in the mare.
Meanwhile, the poised sky opens on rain.
The time on either side of *now* stands fast
glinting like jagged window glass.

There are limits, my God, to what I can heft
in this heat! Clearly, the Great Rat waits,
who comes all winter to gnaw on iron
or wood, and tears the last flesh from the bone.

The Survival Poem

I saw a picture of a market stall in the morning paper and under the picture was written, "The dreaded rutabaga has again made its appearance. . . ." When people talk to me about the Occupation of Paris they mention the dreaded rutabaga.

—MAVIS GALLANT, *A Fairly Good Time*

Welcome, old swede,
old baggy root,
old bindrag as well
of Bonaparte's troops.
When the horses' nostrils
are webbed with ice
and out of the hay
fall torpid mice
and calves go stiff
in their mothers' wombs
and the apple core
cloaks the tunnel worm;
when the soldiers' bandages
hung out to dry
clatter like boards
in the four-o'clock sky
and the last blood runs
from the bulbs of the beets
and the cabbages shed
their hundred sheets,
welcome, old swede,
strong-smelling Bigfoot.
In the camps all ate
from the same rank pot.

Let me dine with praise
on you alone.
Pray the Lord lay me down
one more time like a stone;
one winter more
from my musty bed
pray the Lord raise me up
in the morn like bread.

Notes on a Blizzard

Snow makes Monday as white
at supper as breakfast was.
All day I watch for our wild
turkeys, the ones you've tamed
with horse corn, but only the old
one comes, toeing out on his henna feet.
Small-headed, pot-bellied, he stands
too tall—I need to think this—
to tempt a raccoon. Tonight, not
turning once, I sleep in your empty space
as simply as a child in a child's cot.

Tuesday, the sky still spits
its fancywork. Wherever
the chickadees swim to is secret.
The house breathes, you occur to me as
that cough in the chimney, that phlegm-fall
while the wood fire steams, hard put
to keep itself from going out.

Wednesday, the phone's dead.
The dog coils his clay tail across
his eyes and runs, closing in
on a rabbit. Late afternoon,
in a lull, I go out on snowshoes
to look the woods over.
Above the brook a deer
is tearing bark from a birch tree,
as hungry as that, tearing
it off in strips the way
you might string celery.

Only liars keep diaries.
I didn't see him curling his lip
or the papery festoons pulled free.
Only his backside humping away
clumsily through the deep snow.
Only the half-moon hoofprints refilling
and the cupful of raisin droppings.

Thursday, the wind turns. We're down
to snow squalls now. Last night you walked
barefoot into my dream. The mice
wrangling on all sides
raised thunder in my head,
nothing but lathe and plaster
between them and the weather.

It's Friday. The phone works.
You're driving north. Your voice
is faint, as if borne across
clothesline and tin cans from the treehouse.
The turkeys show up again
flopping under the kitchen window
like novice swimmers daring the deep end.
Low on corn, I offer jelly beans.
The sun comes out eventually,
a bedded woman, one
surprised eye open.

Territory

Mistaking him for a leaf, I cut a toad
in two with the power mower and he goes on
lopsidedly hopping until his motor runs out

his known universe a jungle of inch-high trees
the ferns by the granite ledge as immense
as sequoias, the stone a terrible Andes.

By the next pass there is no sign of my carnage.
Now I have cut a swath around the perimeter
declaring this far the grass is tamed.

I think of the wolf who marks his territory
with urine, and where there is wolf there is
the scientist who follows him, yellowing

the same pines at the same intervals
until the baffled creature, worn out
with producing urea, cedes his five acres.

We are not of it, but in it. We are
in it willynilly with our machinery
and measurements, and all for the good.

One rarely sees the blood of the toad.

How It Goes On

Today I trade my last unwise
ewe lamb, the one who won't leave home,
for two cords of stove-length oak
and wait on the old enclosed
front porch to make the swap.
November sun revives the thick
trapped buzz of horseflies. The siren
for noon and forest fires blows
a sliding scale. The lamb of woe
looks in at me through glass
on the last day of her life.

Geranium scraps from the window box
trail from her mouth, burdock burrs
are stickered to her fleece like chicken pox,
under her tail stub, permanent smears.

I think of how it goes on,
this dark particular bent of our hungers:
the way wire eats into a tree
year after year on the pasture's perimeter,
keeping the milk cows penned
until they grow too old to freshen;
of how the last wild horses were scoured
from canyons in Idaho, roped, thrown,
their nostrils twisted shut with wire
to keep them down, the mares aborting,
days later, all of them carted to town.

I think of how it will be
in January, nights so cold

the pond ice cracks like target practice,
daylight glue-colored, sleet falling,
my yellow horse slick with the ball-bearing
sleet, raising up from his dingy browse
out of boredom and habit
to strip bark from the fenced-in trees;
of February, month of the hard palate,
the split wood running out,
worms working in the flour bin.

The lamb, whose time has come, goes off
in the cab of the dump truck, tied to the seat
with baling twine, durable enough
to bear her to the knife and rafter.

O lambs! The whole wolf-world sits down to eat
and cleans its muzzle after.

The Grace of Geldings in Ripe Pastures

Glutted, half asleep, browsing in
timothy grown so tall I see them
as through a pale-green stage scrim

they circle, nose to rump,
a trio of trained elephants.
It begins to rain, as promised.

Bit by bit they soak up drops
like laundry dampened to be ironed.
Runnels bedeck them. Their sides

drip like the ribs of very broad
umbrellas. And still they graze
and grazing, one by one let down

their immense, indolent penises
to drench the everlasting grass
with the rich nitrogen

that repeats them.

A Mortal Day of No Surprises

This morning, a frog in the bathtub
and not unhappy with his lot
hunkering over the downspout
out there in the pasture.
Strawberries, moreover,
but not the bearing kind, scrub
growth, many-footed pretenders,
running amok in the squash hills and valleys.

Out of here! I say
ripping the lime-green tendrils from
their pinchhold on my zucchini blossoms
and out! with a thrust of the grain scoop
to the teal-blue frog who must have fallen
from the sky in a sneakstorm that slipped
in between two and three a.m. when
even God allows for a nap.

Last night at that sneakstorm time
(God sleeping, me working out
among the old bad dreams),
two white-throated sparrows
woke me to make their departmental claims—
Old Sam Peabody peabody pea—
wrangling like clerks in adjoining bureaus
only to recommence at dawn
saying their names and territories.

Now for good measure
the dog brings in one half a rank
woodchuck no angel spoke up for

but won't say where he's banked
the rest of the treasure
and one of this year's piglets
gets loose again by rooting under,
emerging from mud like a crawfish,
to stumble across the geese's path
and have an eye pecked bloody by the gander.

All this in a summer day
to be gone like cloth at the knees
when the dark comes down
tough and ancient as thistles.
A day predictable as white-throat whistle,
a day that's indistinguishable
from thirty others, except the mare's
in heat and miserable,
squirting, rubbing her tail bare.

When I'm scooped out of here
all things animal
and unsurprised will carry on.
Frogs still will fall into those
stained old tubs we fill
with trickles from the garden hose.
Another blue-green prince will sit
like a friend of the family
guarding the doomspout.
Him asquat at the drainhole,
me gone to crumbs in the ground
and someone else's mare to call
to the stallion.